STORM SURFER

Lisa Trumbauer

illustrated by Tuesday Mourning

Librarian Reviewer
Chris Kreie, Media Specialist

Reading Consultant
Mary Evenson, Teacher

Raintree

www.raintreepublishers.co.uk
Visit our website to find out
more information about
Raintree books.

To order:
☎ Phone 0845 6044371
🖷 Fax +44 (0) 1865 312263
🖵 Email myorders@capstonepub.co.uk

Customers from outside the UK please telephone +44 1865 312262

Raintree is an imprint of Capstone Global Library Limited, a company incorporated in
England and Wales having its registered office at 7 Pilgrim Street, London, EC4V 6LB –
Registered company number: 6695582

"Raintree" is a registered trademark of Pearson Education Limited, under licence to
Capstone Global Library Limited

Text © Stone Arch Books 2009
First published by Stone Arch Books in 2009
First published in hardback and paperback in the United Kingdom by
Capstone Global Library in 2010
The moral rights of the proprietor have been asserted.

Edited in the United Kingdom by Diyan Leake
Original illustrations © Stone Arch Books 2009
Illustrated by Tuesday Mourning
Originated by Capstone Global Library Ltd
Printed in China by Leo Paper Products Ltd

ISBN 978 1 406 21383 6 (hardback)
14 13 12 11 10
10 9 8 7 6 5 4 3 2 1

ISBN 978 1 406 21404 8 (paperback)
14 13 12 11 10
10 9 8 7 6 5 4 3 2 1

British Library Cataloguing in Publication Data
Trumbauer, Lisa – Storm surfer
A full catalogue record for this book is available from the British Library.

Disclaimer
All the Internet addresses (URLs) given in this book were valid at the time of going to
press. However, due to the dynamic nature of the Internet, some addresses may have
changed, or sites may have changed or ceased to exist since publication. While the author
and publisher regret any inconvenience this may cause readers, no responsibility for any
such changes can be accepted by either the author or the publisher.

CONTENTS

Chapter 1 ›
SHARK GIRL

Jenny scanned the ocean. Her legs dangled over the sides of her surfboard. Her board bobbed gently in the water. She was looking for a wave, any wave, that would take her in to shore.

The ocean was way too calm. Definitely not a good surfing day.

Suddenly, a shrill scream burst across the water.

"Shark!"

Jenny quickly turned on her board. She looked in the direction of the warning. Then she shook her head.

"Not again," she said to herself. She lay down on her board and began paddling.

"Shark!" Megan shouted. She waved her arms frantically. "It's not a mistake this time! I swear!"

"Megan!" Jenny called to her. She was still several feet away. "You really have to stop."

Jenny could tell that Megan was panicking. Her eyes were wide, and her legs were drawn up on her board, her knees up to her chin.

She stopped waving when she saw Jenny, and she gripped the edge of her surfboard. Jenny could see that Megan's knuckles were bone white.

Jenny paddled up to her. "You know the story of the boy who cried wolf, don't you? You're going to be known as the girl who cried shark!" she said.

Megan released a shaky hand from her board. She pointed over Jenny's shoulder. "Look!"

Jenny looked where Megan pointed. At first, she didn't see anything. Then she caught a glimpse of something. Something that looked a bit like a shark's fin.

"Stay here," she told Megan. "I'll be right back."

Jenny paddled her surfboard towards the fin-like thing. Two other objects poked up around it. They looked circular. They looked suspiciously like the tubes of snorkelling gear.

Jenny drifted up to one and placed her hand over the top of the tube. Within seconds, a head came spluttering to the surface. "Hey! What did you do that for?" It was Abby Miller. And Jenny was sure the other snorkel belonged to Sarah Roberts.

Sure enough, Sarah's blonde head popped up from the water. "We were just having a little fun," Sarah said.

"That girl is so afraid of sharks, she'll believe anything is deadly," Abby added.

"Even a surfboard!" Sarah said, giggling.

Jenny rolled her eyes. "Whatever," she said.

She watched as Abby and Sarah flipped the surfboard over, hiding its fake fin. Abby lunged on to it, lay on her stomach, and began paddling towards shore. Sarah swam swiftly beside her.

Jenny turned her own board around and headed back to Megan. The scared girl still sat glued to her surfboard.

"See?" Jenny said. "No shark."

"How did you know that?" Megan asked.

Jenny shrugged. "Shark fins are usually much, much bigger."

Megan's eyes widened.

Jenny laughed. "I'm kidding! I could just tell it wasn't a shark. It looked more like the bottom of a surfboard. Come on. Let's go in. The ocean is dead today."

Jenny watched Megan untuck her knees and stretch her legs out along the board.

"Do I have to put my feet in the water? You know, a surfboard looks just like a seal to a shark," Megan said.

Jenny smiled. "You watch too many nature programmes."

Megan finally smiled back, weakly. "Yeah, well, what can I say? I like to research something before I do it."

The two girls started paddling to shore.

"So why are you at surf camp, if you're terrified of the ocean?" Jenny asked.

"I'm not afraid of the ocean. I'm just afraid of sharks," Megan said.

"Well, Cornwall might not be the surfing capital of the world, but I don't think you have to worry about sharks here," Jenny told her. She smiled as they walked on to the beach.

"Famous last words!" Megan said.

Chapter 2 >
THE IDEA

"Everyone! Time to sign up for the camp competition!" Katie said, clapping her hands.

Katie was one of the camp instructors. Tall, thin, tan, and blonde, she looked like a surfer girl.

Jenny and Megan grasped their surfboards under their arms and jogged up the beach. About a dozen other kids gathered around Katie.

Katie stood in front of a wooden stall. Across the top, there was a sign that read, "Surf Camp."

That afternoon, an extra banner flew from the stall. "Camp Competition" flapped in the ocean breeze.

Jenny sighed. The competition was for teams of two. She and her best friend, Mia, had planned to go to surf camp together. Mia's parents decided at the last minute to take a family holiday. Jenny had made plenty of friends during surf camp, but most of the kids were already paired up.

This was Jenny's third summer at the camp. It was supposed to be the summer she and Mia finally won the competition. Now it looked like she'd have to give it a miss.

She saw Abby and Sarah in front of the sign-up line, giggling. Of course they were going to enter. They'd probably win, too.

They weren't the best surfers, but they were the bravest. And sometimes, they were the craziest. Suddenly, Jenny had an idea. She turned to Megan.

Megan was busy twisting her long blonde hair to get all the water out. "I'm so glad we don't have to enter the competition if we don't want to," Megan said. "I think I'll just watch from shore."

Jenny grabbed Megan's arm and pulled her towards the stand. "I don't think so," Jenny said.

"What do you mean?" Megan asked.

"You and me!" Jenny said. "We're going to be a team. And we're going to win!"

Chapter 3 ›
DOUBLE DOSE

The next day, Jenny and Megan waded into the sea. Their surfboards floated in front of them.

"This is a complete mistake," Megan said. "I'm a disaster."

"Tell me again why you signed up for surf camp?" Jenny asked.

"I didn't," Megan explained. "My parents signed me up because I'm on the swimming team at my school."

"So you like the water," Jenny said.

"I do! But I like it in a pool with chlorine and no rocks and no surprises," Megan said, shaking her head.

"I've been swimming here my whole life," Jenny said. "You won't find many surprises in Cornwall either."

"What about riptides? And crabs in the sand? And huge waves?" Megan looked worried.

Jenny laughed. "I wish we could catch a huge wave!" she exclaimed. "We'd win this competition for sure!"

The water lapped around their knees. "Seriously," Jenny said. "Surfing's not all that hard. All you need is a double dose of C."

"The sea?" Megan asked.

"No, the letter C," Jenny explained. "Confidence and courage."

"I don't think I have much of either of those," Megan said.

"Don't worry," Jenny told her. "We won't go out as far as we did yesterday. We'll only go out waist high. That should build your confidence."

"What about the courage part?" Megan asked.

Jenny smiled. "That part will come with practice," she said.

Megan frowned. "Can't we practise on shore, like we did before?" she asked.

"I don't think sand surfing is a sport," Jenny said, smiling. "But if it was, you'd be an expert."

Megan returned Jenny's smile, but it wasn't a big one.

Jenny pushed herself up on to her board and lay flat on her stomach. "Okay, start by getting on the board, like I just did," she said.

Megan slid on to the board. "That's easy," she said. "That's always the easy part."

"Good. Now, push yourself up and swing your feet on to the board, like this." Jenny showed Megan how to land on the board with one foot slightly ahead of the other.

Megan tried to copy her. Instead of landing on her feet, she fell on her knees. The board wobbled, and then it toppled over, taking Megan with it.

Megan splashed back up to the surface. "What am I doing wrong?" she asked.

Jenny straddled the board, her legs hanging over the sides. "You're landing on your knees first, not your feet," she explained. "That can throw you off balance."

"Okay, let me try again," Megan said.

The girls practised for an hour. Katie came over a few times to offer advice. Jenny didn't even think of letting Megan try to catch a wave. She had to be able to stand on the board first.

They stayed in the shallow part of the beach. Further down, Jenny saw the more expert surfers doing their stuff.

She held back a sigh. She wanted to be there. She wanted to catch a wave. She wanted to feel the power of the water beneath her. But she wouldn't leave her new partner.

Still studying the surfers, Jenny narrowed her eyes. Something was off. She'd seen something that just wasn't supposed to be done.

"Come on," she said to Megan. She flipped on to her board and began paddling across the water.

"Jenny, wait!" Megan called after her. "What's wrong?"

"Abby and Sarah!" Jenny said over her shoulder. She paddled harder.

Chapter 4 ›
THE RULES

By the time they reached the group, the argument was full blown. Abby and Sarah stood on the beach, surfboards under their arms.

Two boys and another girl stood in front of them. All of them were dripping wet. One surfboard lay in the sand.

"We did not steal your wave!" Abby said to a boy in long, colourful swimming trunks. "You were just too slow."

Jenny recognized the boy. His name was Ryan, and he didn't go to surf camp. He was a local. He was a few years older than they were. Jenny had seen him the summers before. They'd talked a few times.

"The two of you cut me off," Ryan said. His brown hair dripped into his eyes.

"We didn't cut you off," Sarah said.

Abby nodded. "Yeah," she said.

"Yes, you did," Jenny said, stepping up to the group.

All their heads turned to her. Abby squinted and said, "What do you know about it? You weren't even here."

"I saw you from the beach," Jenny explained. "You broke surfing rule number one."

"Surfing doesn't have rules," Sarah said.

"Not officially," Jenny said. "But everyone knows that you should respect the more experienced surfers. You never steal another surfer's wave."

"We're experienced!" Abby said angrily.

"And we did not steal this boy's wave!" Sarah added.

Jenny shrugged. "That's not how I saw it," she said. "And I bet that's not how they saw it. Right?" She looked at the girl and the boy standing next to Ryan. All three of them nodded.

"See?" Jenny said, turning back to Abby and Sarah.

"What are you, the surfing police?" Abby asked.

Jenny smiled and said, "Hardly! But we don't want to give the surfing camp a bad name."

Abby and Sarah had run out of words. They stared at Jenny a moment longer, then quickly walked off with their surfboards under their arms.

"That was brilliant!" Megan said, standing beside Jenny. "Did you really see them cut him off?"

Jenny nodded. "Sorry about Abby and Sarah," she said to Ryan and his friends. "We're not all like that at surf camp."

"Usually not," Ryan said. "You're Jenny, right? Didn't we meet last summer?"

"That's right," Jenny said. "Good memory!"

"Don't apologize for your friends," Ryan said.

"They're not our friends," Megan said.

"They should show respect," Jenny said. "Those two are always trying to make other people look stupid."

"That's why we're going to beat them in the camp competition," Megan said.

Ryan laughed. "Really? I saw you guys from the beach. You can't even stand up!"

Megan frowned. "I know. Jenny's a pro. And she's really patient. I'm not a bad swimmer. I'm on the swimming team at my school. I just can't get the hang of surfing."

"There's nothing to it!" Ryan said. "You just have to feel the ocean. Pretend the ocean is your friend."

"I think that's the problem," Jenny said. "Megan thinks the ocean is full of things out to get her, like sharks."

"And jellyfish! And stingrays!" Megan shouted.

Ryan and his friends burst out laughing.

"See what I mean?" Jenny said.

"I've got the perfect solution," Ryan said. "We'll have you up on a surfboard in no time."

Chapter 5

SPECIAL TRAINING

"A swimming pool?" Megan said the next day. "You're joking, right?"

"I never joke about surfing," Ryan said.

"It's perfect!" Jenny agreed. "I don't know why I didn't think of it before."

They had arranged to meet Ryan at a nearby water park first thing in the morning, before the park opened. Surfboards were not allowed in the park, of course, but Ryan's uncle was the manager.

When Ryan explained the situation, his uncle agreed to let them in before the park opened.

Megan looked skeptically at the pool. Her surfboard was propped up against a nearby table. "I feel safer in the pool, but I don't know about this," she said.

"We only have half an hour," Ryan said. "But I think that's enough time to get you used to the feel of the board underneath your feet."

"Do you think so?" Megan asked nervously. She looked at Jenny.

"You like the pool, right?" Jenny said. "Now we're just combining the pool with a surfboard."

"And before you know it, you'll be surfing with the best of them," Ryan said.

"Why do you care if I can surf or not?" Megan asked Ryan.

Ryan shrugged. "Let's just say I'd like to see those other two girls put in their place," he said.

* * *

After half an hour, Megan was able to stand on her surfboard. She'd even ridden a few waves, made by Jenny and Ryan moving their hands in the water.

Jenny thought Megan had done pretty well. She was a good swimmer, at least when she wasn't worried about being eaten by sharks. When she fell into the water – which was often – her strokes were smooth and strong. Jenny noticed that Megan didn't hesitate to get wet or put her head under water. In fact, she seemed like a natural.

Now all they had to do was get Megan used to the sea.

Jenny and Megan thanked Ryan and left him at the park. They wanted to get back to camp before anyone realized they'd been gone. Or before anyone realized what they'd been doing.

Jenny just didn't want anyone to know about Megan's extra training, especially Abby and Sarah.

Jenny and Megan walked from the main street on to the beach. As they got closer to camp, they could see that about two dozen kids were standing around the surf camp stall. Katie stood behind it, talking.

When they got closer, Jenny realized something was wrong. Katie was talking slowly. She was not her usual bubbly self.

"What's going on?" Jenny said, nudging one of the boys in their group.

"A big storm," Callum whispered back. "Looks like we'll be grounded in a few days."

"A storm?" Megan said. "When?"

"It's coming in from the Atlantic Ocean," Callum told her. "It's supposed to be here by Friday."

"Friday!" Jenny said. "But that's –"

"That's right, Jenny," Katie said loudly. "That's the day of the competition. Nice of you and Megan to show up this morning."

Chapter 6 ›
A BEAUTY

Twenty heads turned to look at Jenny and Megan. Jenny felt heat crawl up her face. She didn't like to attract attention, especially negative attention. Now she'd have to come up with an excuse for why they were late.

But Megan spoke up. "We're sorry, Katie," she said. "Jenny was just giving me some extra pointers down on the beach. She didn't want anyone to see how bad I was."

"That's not hard," Abby said loudly.

"If you girls had been on time, you would have heard that we're going to have to postpone the surfing competition," Katie said. She sounded annoyed.

"For how long?" Jenny asked.

"As I was just explaining," Katie said, "it's hard to tell. Storms can be very unpredictable. We know it's coming in from the Atlantic, and we know it's going to hit Cornwall. We don't know how strong it will be, and we don't know where, exactly, it will land."

"I think it's exciting," Callum said. "The waves during a big storm are amazing!"

"And dangerous," Katie said. "Once we put up the red flags, I don't want to see anyone surfing. In fact, you shouldn't even be near the water. Is that understood?"

Everyone nodded.

"Good," Katie said. "Now, for those of you who have already mastered how to find and catch a wave, let's work on angling and leaning. The rest of you will work with Jon on perfecting the basics."

Jenny looked longingly at the advanced group of surfers. She could handle the basic stuff in her sleep. But she didn't want to leave Megan.

It was as if Megan were reading her mind. "You should go with them, Jenny," Megan said with a nervous smile. "I'll be fine with the basics class. At least I can stand up on the board now, right?"

Jenny was torn. "If you're sure about that," she said. "You *are* probably in better hands with Jon than with me at this point."

Megan nodded. "Since the competition is postponed, I'll have time for more practice. And you will, too."

Jenny didn't hesitate. "Remember what we did at the pool!" she said. Then she sprinted away. "You'll be great!" she called back.

Jenny liked helping Megan, but as she ran towards the advanced class, she felt free. She dashed into the ocean after the other surfers and slapped her board on top of the water. She threw herself on to her board and paddled towards the small group.

Suddenly, she saw it. A wave. A wonderful, beautiful wave.

It would roll right by the class. Her fellow surfers were sitting on their boards, listening to Katie. They would miss it.

But it would reach her just in time.

Jenny turned her board around and pointed it towards the shore. She began paddling, moving with the motion of the wave, waiting until she could feel it under her. She would wait until she sensed that it was just the right moment.

One more second. One more second.

Now!

Jenny pushed herself up on her board. She put out her arms to steady herself and angled her feet to maintain her balance. She could feel the power of the wave. The wind and spray whipped around her.

Out of the corner of her eye, Jenny saw a flash of movement. A second later, something hurtled into her.

Jenny flew off her board.

Chapter 7 ›
WIPE-OUT!

Jenny knew how to fall. She just didn't like doing it.

She covered her head and dived into the water. She felt the wave pummel her, but the worst part of the wave had already passed. Something tugged her foot, so she knew her surfboard was still attached to its leash cord.

That was good. It would be awful to lose it. It was one of her favourite things.

Lifting her head, she broke the surface of the water. She looked around, trying to spot what had knocked her off her board.

Abby and Sarah were high-fiving down on the beach. Jenny pulled her surfboard towards her, hopped on, and swam to shore.

"Nice ride!" she heard Sarah tell Abby.

"It was a great ride until you ran into me, you mean," Jenny said.

"Was that you?" Abby asked innocently. "I didn't even notice."

"Jenny! Are you all right?" Ryan called as he walked over. He had been surfing further down the beach when Abby and Sarah crashed into Jenny.

"I'm fine," Jenny assured him. "It probably looked worse than it was."

"It looked pretty bad from where we were," Sarah said.

"That was a pretty big wipeout," Abby said.

"That didn't look like a wipeout to me," Ryan said. He looked suspiciously at Abby and Sarah. "From where I was standing, it looked like someone knocked Jenny off her board," he added.

Abby and Sarah giggled softly.

Ryan turned to Abby and Sarah. "You wouldn't know anything about that, would you?" he asked.

"Us?" Abby said innocently. "Nope, we were just surfing. We weren't paying any attention to Jenny."

Then Jon, the basics instructor, walked up. He looked angry.

"Did you run into Jenny?" Jon asked, crossing his arms.

"Of course not," Sarah said.

"We wouldn't be congratulating each other if we'd run over someone, would we?" Abby added.

Jon stared at them. Jenny thought he believed them. "You girls be careful," he said finally.

"Oh, we will, Jon, honest," Abby said.

Jenny watched him walk down the beach. She planned to tell Abby and Sarah just what she thought, but she didn't want to do it in front of an instructor.

When she turned back to Abby and Sarah, though, they were gone. They were in the sea again.

Their legs hung over each side of their boards, and they leaned forwards, talking to each other. Jenny could only guess what they were saying.

"Trying to work out another way to make our lives miserable, probably," she said to Ryan.

"No kidding," he said. "I'm glad you're okay. I have to go. See you later."

Jenny looked at Abby and Sarah again. They liked to make trouble, that was for sure. But they also liked to do their own thing. And Jenny knew that when it came to surfing, that could be dangerous. Very dangerous.

Now, she just needed to work out what their next move was.

Chapter 8 ›
RED FLAGS

Friday morning dawned beautiful and sunny.

If the television in the common room hadn't been constantly set to the weather forecast, no one would have known the storm was coming.

"Radar doesn't lie," Callum said, slouched on a couch along with a few other kids.

Jenny and Megan sat on the other sofa. Abby and Sarah weren't around.

"Why couldn't it have gone further into the ocean?" Jenny said. "The way this thing is heading, the Carolina coast is going to be right in the middle of it."

"I hate to admit that I'm glad," Megan said.

Everyone turned to stare at her.

"I mean, I'm absolutely rubbish at surfing. I need all the practice time I can get before the competition," Megan said quietly.

"You just need confidence," Jenny said. "And courage. In fact, come on. Let's go and build up some confidence and courage and watch the storm come in."

The girls jumped up from the couch and walked outside. Although the sun was out, Jenny could feel the change in the air as the storm came closer.

The wind had picked up a bit, blowing her hair around her face. And the air felt heavy, pushed down by the pressure from the storm.

* * *

By that afternoon, the storm was almost upon them.

"Look at the size of those waves!" Ryan said as they stood on the beach.

Only a few hours before, the sea had been fairly calm. It hadn't even been windy.

Now, Jenny watched the water rise, like the claws of a bear or a dragon, then thunder down on to the beach. As soon as one wave broke, another wave rose up behind it.

It was amazing. But it was terrifying at the same time.

Jenny stood between Ryan and Megan. She looked up and down the beach. Red flags dotted the sand, warning everyone to stay out of the sea.

"Not that we need a red flag to tell us that," Jenny thought. The huge waves were warning enough.

"Now, this is an ocean you should be afraid of," she said, turning to Megan.

"It's wild, isn't it?" Megan said. She took a deep breath. "It feels wonderful!" she said.

"Wonderful? It doesn't seem wonderful to me," Ryan said. "Powerful, maybe. But not wonderful."

"It's so alive!" Megan said.

Jenny couldn't believe it. "You're afraid of sitting on a surfboard in a calm sea, but this doesn't scare you?" she asked.

Megan laughed. "Well, sure, it's scary, but I'm not going in it, am I? It's just so cool to watch!" she explained.

Jenny shook her head, smiling. Megan did have a point. There was something incredible about the wind and the sound of the waves and the splattering of rain that was starting.

Megan grinned. Jenny grinned back, but then Megan's smile turned to a frown. Jenny turned to see what Megan was looking at.

A boy was running up the beach. Jenny recognized Callum's blue swimming trunks, even though he was still too far away to see his face clearly. Something about the way he was running and waving his arms made her stomach lurch.

Something was wrong.

Jenny began sprinting towards him. Megan followed her. When he saw Jenny and Megan start running, Ryan followed them.

"What is it?" Jenny asked when she got close to Callum. "What happened?"

"It's Abby and Sarah," Callum said, panting.

"What do you mean?" Megan asked.

"You've got to come and help," Callum said. He took a huge breath. "They're in the sea, and we can't get them to come out!"

Chapter 9

STUPID!

"Are they hurt or anything?" Jenny asked.

Callum shook his head. "No, but the warning flags are up everywhere. We keep waving and yelling at them, but it's like they don't get it."

"That was so stupid!" Jenny said. She turned to Callum. "Callum, run back to the camp and tell Katie where we are. I don't want to get Abby and Sarah in trouble, but I also don't want them to get hurt."

Callum nodded and took off across the beach.

"Come on!" Jenny said to Ryan. The three of them jogged back the way Callum had come. Soon, Jenny saw a small crowd gathered on the beach.

"I bet they're not here to watch the waves," Megan said.

Jenny looked from the crowd to the sea. Sure enough, Abby and Sarah were out there. The water was so rough she could only catch glimpses of them. She saw Sarah's blonde head. Then she spotted Abby's bright pink bathing costume.

"What are they thinking?" Jenny asked nervously.

"I don't think they are thinking," Ryan said.

Jenny squinted. It was hard to see. The rain was starting to fall harder. The waves were whipping into a frenzy.

Jenny waved her arms, trying to get the girls' attention.

For a split second, she thought she saw them wave back. Then a wave loomed up in front of the two girls, and they disappeared.

"What should we do?" Megan screamed. It was getting hard to hear over the wind.

Just then, someone on the beach yelled, "Look!"

Jenny spun back to look at the sea. Salt water stung her eyes, but she knew what she saw.

Abby and Sarah were both trying to surf on the same wave.

Jenny felt like she was watching it all in slow motion. The two girls lay flat on their surfboards. Then both of them swung their legs up and crouched into a stand. Both girls and boards glided effortlessly, almost like a ballet.

And then one of them wobbled, or maybe it was both of them. One second Sarah and Abby were high above the waves. The next second, they were crashing into each other.

Jenny held her breath. She strained her eyes, trying to see the boards or the girls as they bobbed to the surface. But the sea was too wild. She couldn't see anything.

And then she did see someone out in the water, but it wasn't Abby or Sarah.

It was Megan.

Chapter 10 ›
PARTNERS

"Megan!" Jenny screamed. "Megan!"

Megan didn't turn around. Jenny watched as Megan's strong arms cut sharp, solid strokes across the ocean. Her body rose and fell with the waves.

Jenny ran in after her. Jenny was a good swimmer, but under these conditions, she realized Megan had something she didn't.

Confidence. And courage.

Ryan dived into the water too. Jenny's arms started to get tired as she tried to catch up with Ryan and reach Megan.

Suddenly, Ryan and Megan were right in front of her. Megan had Abby under one arm, and Ryan was holding Sarah.

Jenny grabbed Abby's other arm to help support her. Abby wasn't unconscious. That was a good sign. But she was obviously in pain. She moaned, and Jenny could tell that she would need to see a doctor.

Megan and Jenny dragged Abby on to the beach. They laid her gently in the sand.

When Jenny looked up, she saw Ryan close behind them. Sarah's arm was flung over his shoulder.

Sarah fell next to Abby. She was coughing and sputtering.

Jenny heard sirens in the distance. The ambulances were coming.

Katie ran over to Jenny and Megan. "What happened?" she asked. "Who can tell me what happened?"

Jenny shook her head, too stunned to speak. Other voices rose around her, explaining what had happened.

Jenny turned to Megan, who was kneeling next to her. "I take it back," she gasped.

Megan shivered, and someone put a towel around her shoulders. "Take what back?" Megan asked through chattering teeth.

"You have more confidence and courage than anyone I know," Jenny told her.

Megan smiled. She threw her arms around Jenny and hugged her. "So do you, partner! So do you!" she said.

Jenny hugged Megan back. Then she looked at Abby and Sarah. Paramedics were checking them out.

"Do you think they've learned their lesson?" Megan asked.

"I hope so," Jenny said.

She looked back at the ocean. Suddenly, the competition didn't seem that important anymore. In fact, it didn't seem important at all.

Jenny turned back to Megan. "Let's forget about the competition next week," she said. "It doesn't matter."

"No way!" Megan said. "We're partners, right? We'll give it a shot."

"Only if you want to," Jenny said. "It's really no big deal."

"If you can dive into the ocean in the middle of a storm, then I can definitely try to stand on a surfboard," Megan said, smiling. "Deal?"

"Deal!" Jenny said happily.

The girls helped each other up, and together, they walked down the beach.

ABOUT THE AUTHOR

Lisa Trumbauer is the best-selling author of *A Practical Guide to Dragons*. She's written about 300 books for children, including novels, picture books, and non-fiction books on just about every topic under the sun (including the sun!). She lives with her husband, Dave, two moody cats, and a dog named Blue.

ABOUT THE ILLUSTRATOR

When Tuesday Mourning was a little girl, she knew she wanted to be an artist when she grew up. Now, she is an illustrator who is especially keen on working on books for children and teenagers. When she isn't illustrating, Tuesday loves spending time with her husband, who is an actor, and their son, Atticus.

GLOSSARY

competition contest

confidence strong belief in your own abilities

courage bravery

panic be scared and unable to think clearly

paramedic person who is trained to give emergency care

postpone put off until a later time

pummel punch or hit

riptide strong current flowing away from shore

suspicious as though something is wrong

wipe-out fall

TAKING CARE OF YOUR SURFBOARD

Surfboards are expensive, and they need careful maintenance. If they're taken care of properly, they can last for years. Follow these rules to keep your surfboard in great shape!

1. Don't stand your surfboard against a wall. Invest in a bag to keep your board in so that it doesn't get damaged.

2. Have dings or dents repaired. You can buy a repair kit at a surfboard shop. If you need a quick fix, try using duct tape to cover a dent.

3. Try not to leave your board in the sun. The hot rays can melt the wax and damage your board.

4. Wax helps your feet stay on the surfboard, so make sure that your board always has the proper amount of wax.

SURFING WORDS YOU SHOULD KNOW

The words surfers use are a language of their own! Here are a few surfing words that will help you get started in surf culture.

floater   riding the top part of the breaking wave

peak   central point of the wave

radical   how an extreme move on a surfboard is described

take-off   getting up and standing on the board

tube ride   riding inside a wave. To someone on shore, the surfer is completely hidden until she comes out of the tube of water. The surfer feels like she is covered by a huge tunnel of water!

DISCUSSION QUESTIONS

1. Why do you think Abby and Sarah are mean to the other surfers?

2. Why does Ryan help Megan learn how to stand on her board? What are some other ideas you have that could have helped Meg?

3. At the end of the book, Megan helps Abby and Sarah even though they were mean to her. Have you ever been in a similar situation? What happened?

WRITING PROMPTS

1. At the end of this book, Megan and Jenny are still planning to enter the surfing competition. What do you think happens during the competition? Write a description of how the competition goes.

2. Megan isn't an experienced surfer, but she's a great swimmer. What are the things that you are good at? What are the things that you need to work more on? Make a list of five things you're great at, and five things you'd like to improve.

3. The girls are all attending a surf camp. If you could create the perfect week at a camp, what would it be like? Describe your ideal camp. What would you learn? What would it be called?

FIND OUT MORE

Books

Extreme Surfing, Blaine Wiseman (Weigl
　Educational Publishers, 2009)
Getting into Surfing, Luke and Damien
　Davis (Nelson Thornes, 2008)

Websites

www.britsurf.co.uk
The British Surfacing Association website
has lots of information about surf schools
and competitions in the United Kingdom.

www.cornwalls.co.uk/surfing/
These pages from the Cornwall Guide
website are written by surfers, for surfers.

**www.bournemouth.co.uk/site/things-to-
do/boscombe-surf-reef**
This web page has information on the first
artificial surf reef in Europe.